FRIENDS OF ACPL

j   1983665
Carey, Mary
Owl who loved sunshine

DO NOT REMOVE
CARDS FROM POCKET

ALLEN COUNTY PUBLIC LIBRARY

FORT WAYNE, INDIANA 46802

You may return this book to any agency, branch,
or bookmobile of the Allen County Public Library

DEMCO

D1307128

The Owl
Who Loved
Sunshine

by Mary Carey

pictures by Joe Giordano

GOLDEN PRESS • NEW YORK

Western Publishing Company, Inc.
Racine, Wisconsin

Copyright © 1977 by Western Publishing Company, Inc.
All rights reserved. Printed in the U.S.A.
Golden, A Golden Book® and Golden Press® are trademarks of Western Publishing Company, Inc.
No part of this book may be reproduced or copied in any form without written permission from the publisher.
Library of Congress Catalog Card Number: 76-52894

9029 1

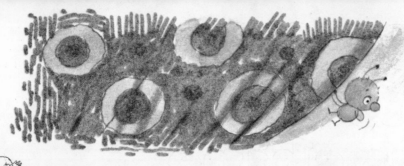

 Chapter 1

Once there was an owl named Leander who lived in the attic of a huge old house on a hill and who wanted very much to be a proper owl.

But Leander wasn't. He wasn't a proper owl at all.

To begin with, he was young. Proper owls are not young. Proper owls are old and wise.

Also, Leander had trouble remembering all the things a proper owl must know and do. There are a great many things that proper owls must know and a great many other things that proper owls must do.

Every afternoon Leander called upon Magellan, an ancient owl who spent his days in the parlor of the big house. When Magellan wasn't dozing on top of a bookcase, he showed Leander charts and maps of the night skies. He pointed out the stars and constellations on a globe so that Leander would know which star was the North Star and which stars weren't.

"Remember the North Star and you'll never get lost when you fly," Magellan said. "You can always find your way home again to your cozy attic."

"I'll remember," Leander promised, and he tried. But he did not always remember. There were so many

stars and constellations that it was hard for a young owl to keep them straight.

After he had visited Magellan, Leander always went to see Plato, the owl who spent his days sitting on the post of the big brass bed in the front bedroom. Plato taught Leander to say "Whooooo?" in a knowing way, as if there were really no need to ask. "And when you sleep," Plato told Leander, "you must always keep your eyes wide open and stare straight ahead."

"Why?" Leander asked.

"Because it's what proper owls do," said Plato. "Besides, staring straight ahead gives owls a chance to think deep thoughts and become very wise."

"I thought it gave us a chance to sleep," said Leander.

"If you're going to be impudent, the lesson is over," snapped Plato.

Leander had not meant to be impudent. He wanted to learn to be proper and owlish. He quickly begged Plato's pardon, and the lesson went on.

5

Leander sat on the brass bed. He stared straight ahead. He tried to think deep thoughts. And he said, "Whoooo? Whooooooo? Whoooo?" until he had it quite right.

Then he flapped off to the dark library, where a truly ancient owl named Horace perched amid dusty papers and dry inkwells and huge, leather-bound books. Horace taught Leander to read about the great owls of history.

One day Leander found a small book, and in it was a poem about an owl and a pussy-cat who went to sea in a beautiful pea-green boat. Horace did not approve of the poem. "He was a foolish owl," said Horace. "Wise owls do not hobnob with pussy-cats."

Leander thought that he must have been a brave owl, just the same, but he did not say so. Instead, he flew back to his attic and perched on his hat rack, where he tried to think only about wise, noble, proper owls. Then he told himself that only one star was the North Star and all the other stars weren't. He said, "Whoooo?" to himself several times, to keep in practice, and he stared straight ahead in a wise and owlish fashion. He hoped that if he kept studying and

practicing and reading and staring and flying abroad with the other owls when they went out at night, he would soon be a proper owl.

But one day all of this ended. One day Leander woke up in the morning, and he saw a sunbeam.

It was coming into the dim, shadowy attic through a chink in the shutters.

Leander had never seen a sunbeam before. He thought it was very pretty, with the dust motes dancing in it. He hopped down from his hat rack and touched it with his claw. It felt warm.

"How nice!" said Leander.

That night Leander flew out with the other owls. He saw the night sky with its thousands of stars, and he remembered which was the North Star. But he also remembered about the sunbeam.

The next morning Leander woke himself up early, just so that he could see the sunbeam again. When it came creeping through the chink in the shutters, he decided that it was even prettier than it had been the day before. Leander wondered if all the world outside his attic was filled with sunbeams. He put his eye to the chink in the shutters and peeked out into the daylight.

The world *was* filled with sunbeams!

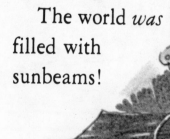

 *Chapter 2*

At first Leander couldn't bear it. The daytime world was so bright that it made his eyes water and he had to look away. He flapped to a trunk that stood at the far side of the attic. There was a pair of spectacles in the trunk, with dark glass in the frames. When Leander put them on, he could look at the sunshine quite comfortably.

Leander opened the shutters and sat on the windowsill. He saw that the sky was blue, instead of black. There were no stars and there was no moon, but there were puffy white clouds. Until now, Leander had seen only dewy meadows that were silver in the moonlight. Now he saw green grass and trees and a sparkling brook. And everywhere, he saw sunshine.

After a time, Leander took off the dark glasses and flew down to the parlor, where Magellan was napping on top of the bookcase.

"Good morning," said Leander timidly.

Magellan opened one eye. "Whoooo?"

"It's me. Leander. That's whooo," said Leander. "I came to find out about something."

"Excellent." Magellan opened both eyes. "What is it?"

"I want to know all about sunshine," said Leander.

"Sunshine?" Magellan quivered from the top of his head to the tip of his tail feathers. "Sunshine? Whatever made you think of sunshine? Sunshine is a dreadful thing! It's . . . it's vulgar!"

"It is?" said Leander.

"All sorts of common creatures go about in the sunshine," said Magellan. "Owls *never* do!"

"Forget that you ever heard of sunshine," ordered Magellan. "And go away. It's too early for lessons."

Leander went back to the attic and closed the shutters. He perched on his hat rack and stared straight ahead, and he tried to sleep, but he couldn't. For now he *was* thinking deep thoughts. He was thinking about the sunshine. He was wondering how sunshine would feel on his wings if ever he dared to fly out into it.

Leander didn't mention sunshine again. But, day after day, he wakened early and watched the dust motes dance in the sunbeams. Then he flew to the trunk and put on the dark glasses, opened the shutters, and looked out at the warm, bright meadow.

13

At last he did fly out. He flew as far as the tall oak tree that stood at the edge of the pond. He found that sunshine was warm on his wings. And he saw that the meadow was a busy place in the daytime.

Birds flitted back and forth, calling to one another. Rabbits tended patches of lettuce and carrots.

Leander saw a pair of meadow mice push a wheelbarrow through the grass. They were gathering seeds.

A comfortable family of squirrels was having a picnic, with hazelnut bread and wild honey set out on a red checked cloth.

Leander saw an old fallen log in the middle of the meadow. A merry, noisy group of youngsters played leapfrog in the clearing around the log. He saw a stout, stern old badger come out to the log and ring a bell. Then the game of leapfrog ended. The young animals trooped across the meadow and into a huge hollow tree trunk. Presently, from the windows of the place, came the faint sound of a little chipmunk announcing that two carrots and two carrots made four carrots.

Leander saw raccoons on the far side of the pond. Some were fishing. Some had crab nets, and they were wading in the shallow water.

There were frogs in the pond, too. They were climbing onto lily pads and diving off again, splashing one another and croaking playfully.

A beaver came out with some twigs and a bucket of mortar. He was going to fix a leak in his dam.

It all looked so nice that Leander stayed in the oak tree until the sun began to set. Then he hurried home to his attic, closed the shutters, and perched on the hat rack. He stared straight ahead and pretended to sleep. The other owls who lived in the house began to stir.

"Come, come, Leander!" called Magellan, the old owl who knew so much about the stars. "It's getting dark. You can't sit there all night."

Leander sighed. He flew to the window and opened the shutters. The sky wasn't blue any more. It was black—a proper night sky for a proper owl. The moonlight had turned the green meadow to silver. All the daytime animals were gone, snug in their tunnels and dens.

That night Leander flew through the darkness with the other owls. He knew the night sky was beautiful, with its sprinkling of stars, but he thought the blue sky of daytime had been even more beautiful. And Leander suddenly felt that the night was cold and empty.

 ## Chapter 3

The next morning, Leander sat on his hat rack and waited for the sunbeam. When it came, he put on his dark glasses, threw the shutters wide, and flew out to the meadow. And there he stayed all the day long, watching the happy, scurrying animals. At sunset he went back to the attic, and when darkness came he flew out with the other owls.

After many days, Leander's eyes grew used to the daylight. He could sit in the meadow without his dark glasses. He was very pleased about this at first, but soon he found out that when he saw well in the daytime, he did not see well after dark.

Proper owls *must* see well after dark.

So Leander had to be careful. He was afraid that he would bump into a tree or a steeple as he was flying.

Leander was tired, too, from staying up all day and flying abroad all night.

He took to falling asleep in odd places.

Once he fell asleep in a church tower. He was there at dawn, when a band of bats returned from their night flight and chased him out.

Once he fell asleep in a barn. A flock of swallows who nested there woke at sunrise and pecked at him.

Several times Leander arrived home in broad daylight. The proper older owls were waiting.

"You were lost!" Magellan would scold. "You forgot to watch the stars!"

"No wise owl is ever out after sunrise!" Plato would tell him. "What *are* you thinking of?"

Leander couldn't tell them he was thinking of sunshine. When the other owls had gone to sleep, he dozed on his hat rack. Sometimes he told himself that he would never again go out into the daylight. "It isn't worth it," he would say. "Besides, proper owls don't do it."

But every day the sunbeam came stealing through the chink in the shutter. And every day Leander remembered the blue sky and the green grass and the warm sunshine and flew out to the meadow.

One afternoon Leander sat too long in the oak tree. He had to hurry to get home before dark. He swooped through the window into the attic.

"Leander!" said a harsh voice from the top of the attic stairs.

It was Magellan.

"Oh, dear!" said Leander.

"You are a disgrace!" declared Magellan.

Leander knew that was true.

"Unnatural owl!" exclaimed old Horace. He was perched on Leander's hat rack, and he looked very angry.

Plato was sitting in the rafters. "Whoooo?" he demanded. "Whooo taught you such tricks? You never learned them from us!"

Leander tried to explain about the sunbeam. He told them about the warm sunshine and the blue sky and the clouds.

"Most improper!" said old Horace. "You must promise that you will never do it again!"

But Leander couldn't promise. He knew that the sunbeam would come into the attic again and that when it did, he would fly out to the meadow.

"Well," declared Horace at last, "if you're so fond of sunshine, you can jolly well get a good dose of it!"

At that, the owls shooed Leander out of the attic and slammed the shutters behind him.

Chapter 4

*A*t first Leander was frightened. It was dark. It was time for owls to spread their wings and ride the night winds. Suddenly he couldn't remember which star was the North Star and which stars weren't. Would he get lost?

But then Leander decided that since he was not a proper owl, he did not have to fly through the night. He could find a new place to perch. He could simply stare straight ahead and forget about thinking deep thoughts. He could stare straight ahead and sleep!

Leander found a tumbledown shed near a deserted farm on the far side of the meadow. There was no comfortable hat rack in the shed, but there was a rusty pitchfork that someone had stuck into the ground and then forgotten. Leander settled himself on the handle. In an instant he was sound asleep. He slept without stirring until dawn.

When he woke up, Leander was hungry. A few small animals were scampering about on the meadow, but Leander did not want to swoop down on them, as an ordinary owl might have done. He felt that they were his friends and that friends did not eat one another. There were sunflowers growing near his shed, and he made his breakfast of sunflower seeds.

After breakfast he was thirsty. He flew to the beaver's pond to get a drink. The beaver saw him coming and slapped the water with his tail. All the frogs who lived in the pond stopped diving and splashing and hid under the lily pads. The beaver dived, too, straight to the underwater entrance to his lodge.

Leander would've liked to have said good morning to the beaver and chatted with the lively frogs. He sighed and had his drink. Then he flew up to the oak tree and sat and watched.

Soon the rabbits came out with their hoes and their spades and began to tend their garden patches.

The raccoons came down to the edge of the stream with their lines and their nets and set about fishing.

The squirrels and the chipmunks and the meadow mice ran back and forth with baskets and barrows and carts and gathered nuts and seeds.

Then the stout old badger who taught in the Hollow Log School rang the bell. From every corner of the meadow young animals came running. The last to arrive at the school was a very small meadow mouse.

Her hair ribbon was crooked, and she was trying to swallow the remains of an acorn muffin as she came.

"Late again, Millicent!" said the badger.

Millicent tried to say that she was sorry, but her mouth was full of crumbs.

"Come, come! Finish your muffin," ordered the badger. "Then, as a reward for oversleeping, you can be the first to recite!"

The badger and the little meadow mouse went into the school and the badger closed the door. Very shortly, Leander could hear the meadow mouse attempting to recite "The Owl and the Pussy-Cat."

Millicent did not really know the poem. She began bravely enough with, "The Owl and the Pussy-Cat went to sea . . ."

That is a far as she got.

"The Owl and the Pussy-Cat went to sea . . ." said the small meadow mouse again.

"Millicent, we know that," said the stern badger. "We want you to tell us what they went to sea *in*."

There was a silence from the schoolhouse.

"Millicent, you did not study," said the badger.

"Poor child," said Leander to himself. He knew what it was to be scolded by someone older. "I'll help her along," he decided, and he flew to perch on the roof of the schoolhouse.

"The Owl and the Pussy-Cat!" he called down the chimney. Then he began to recite in a low, hooting voice:

"The Owl and the Pussy-Cat went to sea
In a beautiful pea-green boat . . ."

"What? What?" The schoolroom door opened and the badger came lumbering out. "What's that? Who's there?" shouted the badger.

"Whoooo?" said Leander. "It's me. Leander. That's whoooo."

The badger looked up. "An owl!" he shouted. "An owl! There's an owl on the roof!"

From the schoolroom came a crashing and a smashing, a thumping and a bumping. It sounded as if scores of young creatures were stuffing themselves into cupboards and hiding under desks.

"Tell them not to be afraid," said Leander. "I won't hurt anyone. I only wanted to help Millicent."

"A likely story!" snapped the badger. "What do you mean, sir, flying about in the daytime?"

"I like sunshine," said Leander.

"Then you are a most unnatural owl indeed," said the badger. He went into the schoolhouse and closed the door. Then he leaned from a window and shouted, "Owl! Owl! Take cover!"

The squirrels and the chipmunks and the meadow mice who were out on the meadow left their barrows and their baskets and their carts and hid in the tall grass. The rabbits dropped their hoes and spades and dodged into their front doors. Even a garter snake, who had been zigzagging lazily across the meadow, raced to hide under a bramble bush.

Leander was alone, sitting atop the schoolhouse.

"Oh, dear!" said Leander. "I only wanted to help that little meadow mouse."

"You mean, you wanted to help yourself to the little meadow mouse," said a whiny voice quite near Leander.

Leander turned to look behind him. He saw a weasel crouching at the edge of the clearing. His bright, hard eyes glittered.

"I'd like to grab that little meadow mouse and gobble her up, too," said the weasel, "but I'd never try it when the badger is around."

"Gobble her up?" cried Leander. "But I won't . . ."

HOLLOW LOG SCHOOL

33

"You certainly won't if you keep spouting poetry down the schoolhouse chimney," said the weasel. "Do what I do. Lay low. Keep quiet. Then grab the young ones when the big ones aren't watching."

The weasel licked his lips.

Leander shivered in spite of the warm sunshine on his feathers.

"You do not belong on this meadow," he began bravely.

The weasel chuckled. "And I suppose you do. Some owl you are, flying around in the daytime!"

"I think you must leave," continued Leander. He trembled inside of himself when he said this, for he was interfering with a day creature. It might not be proper. But the weasel wanted to gobble up young Millicent. Proper or not, Leander knew he had to do something.

So Leander pounced upon the weasel. He seized him and carried him far, far away into the mountains that overlooked the meadow. There Leander found a deep, dark cave. He put the weasel down inside the cave. Then he flew back to the meadow and sat in his favorite oak tree. "I might not be a proper owl," Leander told himself, "but I have helped my friends. I have removed the weasel."

1983665

Chapter 5

*B*ut as the days passed, this was not a great deal of comfort. For, truth to tell, Leander was lonely. Of course the sun was warm and the meadow was beautiful. The sky was blue and the clouds were white and puffy—unless they were gray and filled with rain. Even when it rained, the meadow was pleasant. Leander liked to watch the raindrops patter down into the pond. They always sent the frogs into choruses of joyful croaks. Leander liked to smell the freshness that the rain brought. He liked the clear, cool air that blew across the meadow after a rain.

But Leander wanted to talk to someone about the sky and the clouds and the rain. Above all, he wanted to talk to someone about the warm sunshine.

He couldn't talk to the animals on the meadow. The little ones were terrified of him. They scooted to hide the instant they saw him. The bigger ones didn't trust him and didn't approve of him.

And Leander couldn't talk with the owls, now. No proper owl would have anything to do with him, and besides, they were asleep when he was awake.

So Leander slept in his tumbledown shed at night, and in the daytime he perched in an oak tree. He was sitting in one the morning when the badger came out of his schoolhouse, quite as usual. On that particular morning, the badger did not ring the bell. Instead, he began to nail a poster up on the schoolhouse wall. The poster was almost as big as the badger himself. Leander could read it quite easily from his place in the oak tree.

"HOLLOW LOG SCHOOL FIELD DAY," said the poster. "Sack race! Buttercup relay! High-diving competition! Prizes! Refreshments! Parents invited. Also uncles, aunts, grandparents, and cousins."

It sounded quite exciting.

When the poster was nicely posted, the badger rang the school bell. The young animals came scampering and scurrying across the meadow. The older ones came, too.

The beaver came from his pond and the raccoons stopped their fishing. The beaver supervised while the raccoons put up a grandstand made of popsicle sticks

and odd bits of lumber from old packing crates, all cleverly held together with wooden pegs that the beaver had gnawed from fallen tree trunks.

Two rabbits lugged a rolling pin that was almost as big as they were to a mossy spot near the grandstand, and they rolled the ground smooth.

"I think they're making a racecourse," said Leander to himself. Leander knew about racecourses. He had read about them in one of the books in the library of the old house on the hill.

"The band!" cried the badger suddenly. "Where's the band?"

Half-grown meadow mice and young chipmunks straggled from all corners of the meadow. Some of them were piping shrill notes on reeds they had cut from the edges of the pond. Some of them blew on trumpet flowers. Some of them had stretched lily pads over empty dixie cups to make drums.

"Fine, fine, fine!" said the badger. "Now go over by the bramble bush and rehearse."

The members of the band ran off, piping and tooting and beating on their drums.

The badger looked around. "Sacks?" he said. He seemed hot and fussed and worried. "Where are the sacks for the sack race?"

A plump ground squirrel hurried up with a pile of sacks in her arms. Little Millicent, the meadow mouse, trotted behind her with another pile.

There were paper sacks and burlap sacks and even some cloth sacks that had once held such things as rice and sugar.

"Very good," said the badger. He patted Millicent on the head and smiled at the ground squirrel. "Where did you get these?"

"In the kitchen of the old farmhouse," said the squirrel.

"And the place where humans stop for their picnics," said Millicent.

"Excellent!" said the badger. "The paper ones won't do. Not strong enough for a race. But the burlap sacks are first-rate, and the cloth ones are really fine. Put them over there."

The badger pointed to the clearing near the schoolhouse where a pair of squirrels were putting up a refreshment stand. Little Millicent put the sacks down near the stand—all but one. That one was a lovely cloth sack that had the words DRIED BEANS printed on it.

Leander saw Millicent step into the sack and pull it up around herself.

"That's too big for a tiny animal like Millicent," thought Leander. "But it *is* the nicest sack."

And Leander forgot that he was lonely. He watched Millicent hop to and fro and back and forth with the sack held up around her.

"Look at me, Mama!" cried Millicent. "Look at me! I'm going to win the sack race." With that, she tripped and fell down.

"You'd do better with a smaller sack," said her mother. Her mother wasn't really watching. She was painting some acorns with silver paint so they would look like little silver cups. And if Millicent was having trouble with the big sack, her mother was having

more trouble with her big can of silver paint. She was getting more on the grass and the bushes and herself than she was on the acorns.

"I could paint those acorns easily," said Leander to himself. But he didn't stir. He would have loved to have been part of the hustle and bustle of the meadow, but he knew that if he so much as moved a wing or blinked an eye, he would frighten all the animals back into their burrows and holes and nests. So Leander stayed where he was, and he watched.

He watched the youngsters in the band tune their instruments and play a lively, squeaking march.

He watched the young rabbits form a bucket brigade to fill a chipped teacup near the schoolhouse with water from the beaver pond.

He watched the frogs come leaping across the meadow and climb a ladder to the schoolhouse roof. Then they began to practice high dives from the roof into the cup.

"Remarkable!" said Leander to himself. "They could dive into the pond instead of dragging water up here. Still, diving into a teacup must be rather special. Any old frog can dive into a pond."

HOLLOW LOG SCHOOL

"Buttercups!" shouted the badger. "Do we have enough buttercups?"

The very smallest, very youngest animals dashed off and began hastily picking buttercups for the buttercup relay. Leander listened to the badger explain this race. One young animal would carry a buttercup part of the way around the race course and then pass it to another young animal, who would carry it a bit farther and pass it to a third young animal, who would then pass it to a fourth. The fourth animal would pass it to the last runner, who would run for the finish line. Any contestant who dropped a buttercup would be out of the race. The first runner to reach the finish line would win silver cups for himself and his team.

"Are we ready?" said the badger at last.

They were ready.

49

Chapter 6

"Take your places!" called the badger.

The parents and grandparents and uncles and aunts and cousins scrambled into the grandstand, and the badger disappeared into his schoolhouse. In a moment he was back again. Now he wore an elegant ribbon across his chest. It had words lettered on it with gold paint. "Judge and Chief Official," they said.

"We will begin!" said the badger, in his most official voice. He rang the school bell. "The grand march, please!" he called out.

The meadow mice and the young chipmunks who had been tootling and drumming behind the bramble bush hastily formed themselves into lines. A somewhat older chipmunk carried a lollipop stick all twisted around with tinsel. It looked very grand. He was the bandmaster. He raised his baton into the air, then brought it down again.

The band began to play. The pipers and the drummers and the trumpeters paraded out proudly.

When they reached the schoolhouse steps, the chipmunk waved his baton back and forth in the air. The band stopped, looking proud and out of breath.

"Welcome, everyone, to the Hollow Log Field Day!" said the badger. "We are here to have a good time."

The other animals clapped.

"We are here to enjoy ourselves," said the badger.

The crowd cheered and waved.

"Refreshments have been donated by the Parents Committee," said the badger. "Please feel free to patronize the refreshment stand between the events."

Leander would have liked to have visited the refreshment stand. He felt a bit hungry with nothing but sunflower seeds in his stomach. But he knew that if he moved, the field day would be over before it even began. So he sat perfectly still, and the badger announced that the first event would be the high dive.

All of the frogs swarmed up the ladder to the schoolhouse roof. One after another they threw themselves gleefully into the air. They did back flips and front flips and swan dives and jackknives. One small frog who hadn't been at it very long simply jumped into the teacup feet first.

The badger awarded a silver cup to the frog who did the best back flip, and another to one who did a marvelous jackknife. And the little frog who jumped feet first into the teacup got a prize, too. It was a pretty, gold-colored safety pin that the badger had been saving for some special occasion. The young frog happily tied it around his neck with a bit of thread and hopped off to join his relatives in the grandstand.

After the diving contest, the smallest animals on the meadow took their places along the racecourse that the rabbits had made. The badger handed buttercups to four tiny squirrels. "Ready! Set! Go!" cried the badger, and the squirrels scampered away.

Part of the way around the course, the squirrels handed their flowers to four little mice. Away dashed the mice, with their parents and grandparents and aunts and uncles shouting from the grandstand. One tiny mouse stubbed his toe on a dandelion root and tumbled tail over nose and dropped his buttercup. A great moan went up from the mice in the grandstand, and the tiny mouse who had dropped the buttercup picked himself up and left the racecourse.

The three mice who were left passed their buttercups to three eager little rabbits. Off hopped the rabbits, as fast as they could go, and soon they handed their buttercups to three excited chipmunks. The chipmunks passed the buttercups to three young raccoons.

The raccoons ran for the finish line, where the badger waited with a flag made of black and white checked gingham. The crowd cheered and shouted,

"Run, Roberta, run!" and "Step on it, Alvin!" and "You can do it, Petey!"

In the end, it was the young raccoon named Petey who did it. Three feet from the finish line he managed an extra burst of speed. He dashed across the line inches ahead of the others. The badger dropped his flag and the raccoon handed his buttercup to the badger.

Petey and the members of his team were given silver trophies for their prizes. The raccoons were delighted. And because Petey's team included one squirrel, one meadow mouse, one rabbit, and one chipmunk, almost every animal in the stands had reason to be proud.

Chapter 7

"And now, ladies and gentlemen!" cried the badger. "The big event of the day. The sack race!"

The crowd stopped cheering and grew quiet. The sack race was the hardest race of all. There would be only one winner in the sack race.

"Wait and see," said one elderly bunny to the squirrel sitting next to him. "A rabbit will win. Rabbits always win the sack race."

It did seem likely to Leander that a rabbit would win. Rabbits were excellent at hopping. And though little Millicent had been practicing, bouncing about in her big sack, Leander did not think that she could leap faster than the rabbits.

Now she was taking her place with the other little creatures at the starting line. All had sacks that they held with their forepaws. Seven rabbits had entered the race, and there were two raccoons. Three young squirrels were having trouble keeping their bushy tails tucked inside their sacks. Two chipmunks were squeaking and chattering and taking little practice hops.

Then, "Ready! Get set! Go!" cried the badger.

The grown-up squirrels in the grandstand chattered with glee when a young squirrel named Steve took the lead. But then a bunny named Hortense hopped forward to overtake Steve.

"I knew it!" cried the old rabbit. "A rabbit will win!"

"A rabbit always wins!" shouted another rabbit.

But Millicent was hopping in her sack as fast as a meadow mouse can hop. Her hair ribbon had come untied, but she didn't care. Her sack *was* too big for

HORTENSE

STEVE

FLOUR

RICE

DRIED BEANS

59

her, but she didn't let that slow her down. She clutched the sack as tight as she could, and she gritted her teeth and hopped.

She passed the other meadow mice and the chipmunks. She passed the raccoons. She passed the bounding, leaping rabbits and the speedy squirrels.

"And in a great big sack, too!" said her mother proudly. "Millicent is a great hopper . . ."

But her mother stopped there. For she had glimpsed something at the far end of the racecourse that made her gasp and clutch at Millicent's father.

From his hiding place, Leander saw something, too. There was a patch of tall grass beside the course about a hundred feet from the starting line. It was a hundred feet from the stout old badger and the excited parents and uncles and aunts. Something was moving in that patch of grass.

"The weasel!" cried Leander. "That horrid weasel is back!"

"Millicent! Stop!" shouted her mother.

Too late! The weasel streaked out of the grass and pounced. He picked up the sack, Millicent and all, and he began to make off with the little meadow mouse.

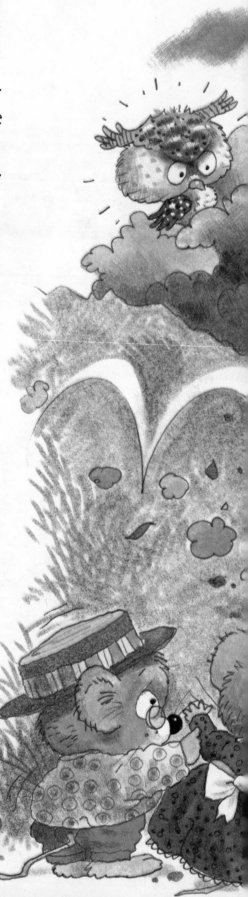

DRIED BE

Millicent's mother and father screamed and shouted, but it didn't help. The badger began to race down the course to catch the weasel, but the weasel was too far away to care about parents, or badgers, either.

He had forgotten about Leander.

Leander spread his mighty wings and soared across the meadow. He passed the grandstand. He passed the panting, sputtering badger. He passed all the small animals on the racecourse. He swooped toward the ground just as Millicent bravely seized a daisy and held fast to its stem. She managed to pull herself out of the sack, which the weasel had in his teeth.

"Wretched child!" snarled the weasel. He dropped the sack and reached for Millicent. And suddenly, there was Leander.

"Oh, no!" cried the weasel. "Not you again!"

The parents and the grandparents and the uncles and the aunts in the grandstand did not know *what* was happening. At first it looked to them as if at least four owls and three weasels were fighting out there on the meadow. The weasel dodged and struggled and squirmed and cried and tried to bite Leander. And Leander flapped and clutched and flew upward and down again and tried to get a grip on the weasel.

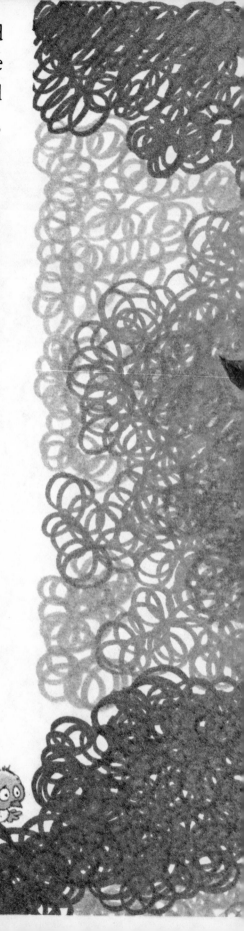

63

Millicent scooted down the racecourse. "Mama! Papa! Help!" she screamed.

Leander wanted to tell her that everything would be all right, but he didn't have time. "First things first," said Leander to himself.

And then at last he fastened one great talon on the weasel's hindquarters and the other on his shoulders. He picked the weasel up and carried him high, high into the air.

"Stupid!" yelled the weasel. "I'd have shared that little meadow mouse with you."

Leander didn't answer.

"Hey!" said the weasel. "Aren't we flying too high?"

"The higher the better," said Leander.

"You. . .you aren't going to drop me, are you?" said the weasel.

"Not right away," said Leander.

He flew over the beaver's pond to the place where the stream ran swift and deep, and there he *did* drop the weasel.

WHOOO

The weasel sank in the fast-running water. He came up and sputtered and sank again. Then he came up and snatched a stick that was floating along. He was carried down the stream and out of sight, shouting and whining and saying some very nasty things about Leander.

Leander laughed a low, hooting laugh, for he knew that weasels don't like water. And he thought that it was quite possible that the weasel might float on forever—or at least until he came to the place where the stream emptied itself into the sea.

Leander flew back to the oak tree and settled himself to wait until the meadow creatures had gotten over their fright. He wanted to watch the rest of the field day.

But there was no more field day.

The youngsters in the band threw down their instruments and trooped toward Leander's tree.

The parents and grandparents and uncles and aunts almost trampled one another in their hurry to get out of the grandstand and thank Leander.

Millicent's parents wept with joy and hugged Millicent tight.

The stout, stern old badger stood opening and closing his mouth for a minute, as if he couldn't decide what to say or what to do. But then he did the proper thing. He walked to Leander's oak tree, and the other animals stepped aside to make way for him.

"I have been mistaken about you," said the badger.

Leander thought this over. Then he nodded an owlish nod. "Perhaps you have," he told the badger.

"You aren't an unnatural owl at all," said the badger. Leander did not remind the badger that he was not an ordinary owl. Any other owl would have gobbled up Millicent *and* the weasel, too.

"Please accept my apologies," said the badger.

"Of course I will," said Leander.

The badger then turned to the other animals and made a very grand speech. He told the daytime creatures that Leander was a noble and courageous owl. And from his schoolhouse the badger fetched a handsome medal, which he presented to Leander. "It's a medal for heroes," said the badger. "It's been in my family for years. That is. . .er. . .I've had it for quite a long time."

Leander could read at least as well as the badger, if not better. He saw that the medal wasn't exactly for heroes. It was a prize that someone had once won in a spelling contest. Leander suspected that the badger had found it at the place where humans sometimes stopped for picnics. But he was delighted to have it, and he knew he would wear it always.

And he did.

He wore it when he presented little Millicent with the silver cup for taking first place in the sack race. The badger had insisted that Leander present the trophy, and Leander had decided that Millicent deserved it. True, she had not really won the race, but none of the other animals had, either.

Leander wore the medal in the days that followed, when he sat in the oak tree and watched Millicent and her brothers and sisters playing in the tall grass.

He wore it when he watched the squirrels harvesting their acorns and the rabbits tending their garden patches.

He wore it when he went to the pond to chat with the lively, croaking frogs.

He wore it in the golden afternoons when he and the badger played chess in the clearing beside the schoolhouse.

He wore it whenever he was invited to dinner by one of the meadow creatures—and this happened at least once every day and twice on many Sundays.

Leander knew that he was not a proper owl. Not proper at all. But he felt very wise, just the same. And he *was* wise, even if he had almost forgotten how to say "Whooooo?" in a very knowing way, like the dusty, proper old owls in the dusty old house on the hill. He knew that nothing made him happier than sunshine on his feathers. Unless it was having friends.